Hit Squad

James Heneghan

orca soundings

ORCA BOOK PUBLISHERS

I would like to acknowledge Bruce McBay's
considerable contribution to this book.
—J.H.

Library and Archives Canada Cataloguing in Publication

Heneghan, James, 1930-
Hit squad / James Heneghan.
(Orca soundings)

ISBN 10: 1-55143-269-2 / ISBN 13: 978-1-55143-269-4

I. Title. II. Series.
PS8565.E581H57 2003   jc813'.54   c2003-910687-x
PZ7.H3865HI 2003

First published in the United States, 2003
Library of Congress Control Number: 2003105879

Summary: Students in an upscale high school decide to take on the bullies and
take back their school, with decidedly mixed consequences.

MIX
Paper from
responsible sources
FSC® C004071

ANCIENT FOREST ™
FRIENDLY

*Orca Book Publishers is dedicated to preserving the environment and has
printed this book on Forest Stewardship Council® certified paper.*

Orca Book Publishers gratefully acknowledges the support for its publishing
programs provided by the following agencies: the Government of Canada through
the Canada Book Fund and the Canada Council for the Arts, and the Province of
British Columbia through the BC Arts Council and
the Book Publishing Tax Credit.

ORCA BOOK PUBLISHERS
PO BOX 5626, Stn. B
Victoria, BC Canada
V8R 6S4

ORCA BOOK PUBLISHERS
PO BOX 468
Custer, WA USA
98240-0468

www.orcabook.com
Printed and bound in Canada.

16 15 14 13 • 11 10 9 8

For my granddaughter Margaux.

Chapter One

Friday afternoon, ninth-grade art class, final period.

Two girls spat sunflower seeds at the blue-eyed blond.

Birgit Neilsen, the blond girl, tossed her ponytail. "Cut it out!" She shook the sticky seeds from her hair and spun around to face her tormentors. "Slobs!" Her eyes were like ice.

The girls at the next bench, Shelley Crewell and Mona Teasedale, eyed each other in mock horror.

"Did you hear that, Shell?" said Mona, the bigger girl. Black mascara circled her eyes. She looked like a raccoon.

Shelley acted shocked. "Ooooh, Mona!" Shelley's dark hair was streaked with a single white skunk stripe across the top of her head from front to back.

Mona said, "She called us slobs! We're not slobs, are we, Shell?"

"No, Mona, we're not! If anyone's a slob around here it's Miss Superior. If you ask me…" Shelley whispered into Mona's ear.

Mona's laughter erupted in a spluttering giggle that sent a spray of wet sunflower seeds into Birgit's hair.

"You two animals belong in a zoo," Birgit hissed. She snatched up her work and moved out of range.

"It's not me," Shelley lied. "I'm eating a Mars bar. Look!" She held up a chocolate bar, still in its wrapper. Her eyes were wide and innocent.

"What's the trouble here?" The art teacher was a big man with a beard and brown hair that fell below his collar. "Shelley? Mona? You planning on working today?"

Except for their jaws, the two girls didn't move. They chewed sunflower seeds.

"Well?"

"Sure, Mr. Paddock." Mona eased her feet off the stool and slouched against the bench. Shelley followed suit with exaggerated slowness.

"And sunflower seeds are forbidden in here. You know that. Stay behind after class and clean that mess off the floor." As Mr. Paddock moved away, Mona jerked a finger at his retreating back. Shelley sniggered.

On the bench next to Mona and Shelley, a girl named Jessie Jones was busy making tiny clay pellets. She fired them through a pen barrel at a boy named Dietrich Mueller, two rows in front of her. She wore a reversed baseball cap and a T-shirt that had *Kill!* written in black letters on it.

Dietrich turned and grinned. "Who keeps doing that?" he asked, looking at everyone behind him. He looked at Jessie. "It's you, isn't it?" He giggled.

Jessie looked innocent. "Deet? You talking to me?"

Dietrich giggled again. "I know it's you, Jess. I know it's you." Dietrich didn't fully understand why people called him Deet. He thought it was simply a friendly way of saying his name. He didn't know that it was the common name of an insect repellent. "How are the flies today, Deet?"

kids asked him. Dietrich always laughed, thinking they were being friendly. Deet was a friendly boy.

Jessie answered, "It's not me, Deet. Must be the mosquitoes, huh?"

Deet laughed and went back to his clay sculpture.

Jessie looked at Shelley. "What's with her highness there?" She nodded in Birgit's direction.

"You mean Miss Superior? She thinks she's too good for the rest of us," said Shelley. "Called us slobs. Ain't that right, Mona?"

"We should teach her a lesson," grunted Mona.

"Yeah, why not?" said Shelley. "We Creekside girls gotta stick together."

"Get her in the stockroom," Jessie suggested.

"And then what?" asked Mona.

"Paint her pretty colors," laughed Shelley.

"You gotta get her in the stockroom first," said Jessie. "Leave her to me, okay?" She headed for Birgit's bench. "I saw what they did, Birgit," she said. "The sunflower seeds, I mean. You're right. They are a couple of slobs."

Birgit didn't look up from her work. "Forget it."

Jessie acted friendly and concerned. She gently brushed a few seeds off Birgit's back. "Birgit, do you know where in the stockroom they keep the paper towels? My bench just ran out."

"They're in a cardboard box at the back beside the…"

"Be a sweetie and help me find them?"

Birgit stopped working and looked around. Mona was busy joking with Shelley. She shot a glance at the other students. Normal. Her hands were covered in wet clay. She tore paper towels off the roller. Wiping the clay from her hands, she followed Jessie to the stockroom.

Mona and Shelley were fast. They quickly followed Jessie and Birgit into the room and closed the door behind them. Mona looped an arm around Birgit's neck from behind and pulled her backward to the floor. Jessie stuffed a wad of paper towels into Birgit's mouth before she could cry out.

"Hold her, Jess!" said Shelley.

Jessie kneeled on one of Birgit's arms. Mona kneeled on the other arm. Shelley sat on Birgit's hips. For Birgit, struggle was useless; the weight of the three ninth graders was too much for her. She waited, ice-blue eyes glaring up at her attackers.

"Get the paint, Shell," said Mona.

"I've got a better idea," said Shelley. "What Miss Superior needs is some nice hot chocolate." She tore the wrapper off her Mars bar and took a bite. "She called us animals, remember?" She passed the bar to Mona.

"And slobs!" said Mona. Her dark eyes glittered through her bandit mask of mascara and eye shadow. She took a bite of her friend's chocolate bar.

Shelley chewed noisily. Then she opened her mouth and drooled sticky saliva-melted chocolate and caramel onto Birgit's upturned face.

Birgit tried to turn away, but they held her head tight. The brown liquid dripped into her hair and dribbled down her cheeks.

Mona copied her friend. She leaned over and slobbered chewed chocolate into Birgit's eyes. Bubbled it out slowly from the sneer of her lips. She made retching noises deep down in her throat.

Jessie laughed nervously. "Gross."

Birgit tried to wrestle her head away. Eyes closed tight. Neck muscles straining.

Jessie grabbed a handful of hair and forced her head straight.

Birgit lay quietly, almost relaxed, taking whatever else they had to give without flinching. Jessie removed her fingers from her hair. Birgit lay still, as if she were dead.

It was quiet in the stockroom. The sounds of the class just outside the door were far away. A single bare lightbulb shone from the ceiling. The floor was black and white squares, like a chessboard. It was narrow, with just enough room for Birgit's spread-eagled body. The room smelled of paint and thinner.

Mona leaned close to Birgit and spat in her ear. "So who's the animal now, huh?"

"Yuck!" said Jessie, screwing up her face in disgust.

The bell rang. The three attackers fled. Birgit's skin was no longer white and her hair was no longer shining.

She pulled the wad of paper from her mouth and sat up, trembling.

A shadow filled the doorway. She looked up through saliva, chocolate and tears. The art teacher stood at the door. His mouth was open as he stared down at her in disbelief.

Chapter Two

Grandview High, Monday, lunch hour.

"Gimme your lunch, kid!"

Mickey Cord, reaching into his locker for his bag lunch, turned to see who was growling in his ear.

"You deaf? Hand over your lunch."

There were two of them. Overweight bullies with mean eyes. The kind who got fat eating other kids' lunches as well as their own. They looked like seniors. They were big. One of them was glaring down at Mickey. The other mountain of lard was hitting the kid in the next locker over.

There were eighth and ninth graders all around. Slam of metal doors. In and out of their lockers. Pretending not to notice what was going on right under their noses. Minding their own business.

Mickey left his lunch in the locker and backed away a few inches. He closed his locker door but kept his hand on it. Fatso moved after him, pushing his big face into Mickey's. Mickey let him have it. He slammed the locker door into Fatso's face. Fatso screamed and staggered backward holding his nose.

"Sorry," said Mickey. "Hand slipped."

A punch came at him from nowhere, landing on his ear. It was Fatso Two coming to the aid of Fatso One.

Mickey fell to the floor, his ear ringing with pain.

Fatso One, his nose leaking blood, came in with the boot to Mickey's ribs. Mickey took the kick and rolled away to avoid a second.

Then suddenly all was quiet. Mickey staggered to his feet. The kid from the next locker was sitting slumped on the floor, his face white. The two Fatsos had disappeared, scared off by the appearance of a teacher, Miss Harlan, heading their way.

Mickey turned toward his locker. His lunch was gone. "They get yours too?" he asked the kid on the floor, an eighth grader by the looks of him.

The boy nodded.

Mickey said, "You okay?"

"Punched me in the stomach. I feel a bit sick. But I'll be okay."

"Is anything wrong?" asked Miss Harlan. "I thought I saw a scuffle."

"Everything's fine," said Mickey, closing his locker loudly.

The kid stood. "Everything's fine."

Mickey and the kid moved away. Mickey's ear was still ringing, and his ribs hurt where Fatso One had kicked him. He said, "You want to come down to the cafeteria? I'll buy you a Coke."

The kid tried to smile. "Thanks."

Tuesday morning, homeroom class.

Mickey found a letter on his desk. It had no stamp. A plain sealed envelope with a letter inside. His name scrawled on the front: *Michael Cord, Division 5, Grade 9, Room 106*.

Michael. That was funny. No one ever called him Michael, even though it was his proper name. Michael was fancy, Grandview High fancy. Mickey. That was what everyone called him, just plain Mickey. If he told the other kids at Hobbit House that Michael was his proper name, they would laugh.

Mickey never got letters, stamped or unstamped. It was something new. He stared at the envelope while the teacher checked attendance. When homeroom was over he shoved it into the hip pocket of his jeans and moved to English class. He settled himself in his usual back seat near the window. He took out the envelope and opened it carefully with a fingernail. One sheet of lined notebook paper. The writing was bold, dashed off with a confident speed. It had exclamation points like bursting grenades.

Michael Cord!
You are invited to a special meeting of my Special Secret Society!
The time: Noon! (Bring your lunch!)

The day: Friday, Oct. 11!
The place: Old band room in the basement!
Purpose of society: It's a secret, dummy! Come and find out!
Warning: Tell nobody else of this meeting!
Come alone!
Destroy this letter!
Birgit Neilsen

Birgit Neilsen. Mickey had heard the name before. Heard people mention her around the school. The only thing he knew about her was that she was from around here, from Grandview. One of the rich kids. Why would a well-off Grandview girl invite him to a special secret society? He was a nobody from Creekside. It didn't figure.

Back when he was at Creekside Junior High he had belonged to a gang. They called themselves the Creekside Cougars, but the gang was pretty harmless. They skateboarded in deserted places late at night. Like the steps of the Vancouver Art Gallery. They skipped school. They sneaked into the movies for free. Big stuff. The worst thing they ever did was break into a store occasionally to steal cigarettes.

But a gang member everyone called Hulk was a real criminal. Hulk spent time in the slammer. He was the oldest and biggest member of the Cougars. Hulk wasn't too bright. The others let him think he was the leader of the gang because it made him feel important. He was big and reckless and he did whatever the other kids wanted him to do.

Mickey was the youngest and smallest member of the Cougars. They occasionally got into real fights with kids from Grandview High who cruised Creekside in their parents' cars. Mickey didn't like fighting. In fact he hated it.

But because he was small he had to act much tougher than he felt. It was all phony. They called him Suicide because he rushed into fights with his head down, eyes closed, fists swinging. He never let on to the others that he wasn't the brave and fearless fighter they thought he was. He rushed into fights because he was scared. But he was even more scared of being seen as a coward.

But that was then. The old days. The gang eventually broke up. Charlie Simms moved to Surrey. Greg Spalenka moved to Manitoba. The others quit their skateboards and took up snow-boarding on the local mountains instead. Hulk's real name turned out to be Hector Coggin. He did a couple of months in a minimum-security prison somewhere out in the Fraser Valley and then they sent him back to Hobbit House. He now lived in Hobbit House with Mickey and a few other foster kids.

Mickey used to envy the well-off Grandview kids. Then the Vancouver School Board did away with the old district boundaries, so with a whole bunch of other kids he registered at Grandview in September. He started riding his bike the two miles each way every day. He wasn't sure exactly why he had bothered to switch schools. Most of the Creekside kids preferred to walk the few blocks to their own local high school, but there were many who just wanted a change. Or they did it because they could. But Mickey set his mind on Grandview with a vague idea of bettering himself somehow. He had the idea that Grandview, because it was a rich area, would be a better school. He wanted to BE somebody. Wanted an education. Then he could get a good job and own his own car. Grandview just seemed like the logical place to start.

He soon discovered that switching to Grandview hadn't made him one of them.

Most of the Grandview crowd acted kind of superior. They could tell he wasn't one of them. Even though he made the football team he was still an outsider. He was still a kid from the East Side. He was still a kid who cycled to school in all kinds of weather. Who at Grandview would ever want to be friends with a kid who rode a bike to school when almost everyone else owned a car or, if they were under sixteen, had their parents drive them to school? Whenever he was in the dressing room with the other guys on the team, they just carried on like he wasn't there. He didn't fit in. It was like he was the invisible man.

He took another look at the letter. Birgit Neilsen. Nice name. But did he really want to join a special secret society? No. He was at Grandview to get an education. Over and out.

He stared at the letter.

But surely there'd be no harm in checking things out, would there? He could go to the meeting simply to peek into that exclusive world of smart, well-off Grandview kids. Simple curiosity, that was all it would be. An outsider looking in. No harm in that.

Life lessons, you might say.

Chapter Three

The next morning, Wednesday, Joey Washington was beaten up in a school washroom. He was whisked to Emergency at the Vancouver General.

Mickey knew Joey pretty well, an eighth grader from Creekside. He was in the Cougars for a short time, a good fighter—fast with his feet. But then his dad found out and made him quit.

Everyone in the gang liked Joey. Nowadays he took the bus up the hill to Grandview every day. He told Mickey he just wanted a change: he was sick of Creekside. Also, Grandview had a big computer lab. He liked working with computers. Grandview parents supplied the money for them, he told Mickey. Creekside had only six computers for the whole school.

Now Joey's face looked like it had been pushed into a meat grinder. And he had broken bones. Poor Joey. It made Mickey mad just to think of it.

Joey was still on Mickey's mind a couple of days later as he shouldered his way along the crowded hallway. He pushed through the cell phones and Walkmans, and out into the yellow October sunshine. He planned to enjoy his lunch under the trees. The grass was littered with horse chestnuts. He kicked absently at spiky green shells and opened up his lunch bag. He was still thinking of Joey Washington, unable to get the picture out of his head of Joey lying broken on the washroom floor.

He started to take a bite out of his cheese-and-tomato sandwich and then remembered it was Friday, the day of the secret meeting. How could he have forgotten? He pushed the sandwich back into the bag and hurried across the grass to the band room in the school basement.

The meeting was just starting. There was one girl and a couple of the guys from the football team.

"Glad you could make it, Michael," said the girl. "I'm Birgit Neilsen. Find yourself a seat and I'll explain why I invited you all to come."

Michael. There it was again. The name. And coming from this classy Birgit girl it sounded to Mickey like music. She sat on an oak desk, leaning back on her hands.

Her slim, designer-jean-clad legs were crossed. Long blond hair tied back in a no-nonsense ponytail. White shirt under a light blue cashmere sweater. Up-market. White Thorlo socks. Two-hundred-dollar Reeboks. No makeup that Mickey could see. She didn't need it.

And he knew her. Knew that face from way back, from what? Two or three years ago? That was the first time he ever saw her, a blond kid in a car. He had never forgotten that face.

Now he knew her name: Birgit Neilsen.

It had been a night in late spring or early summer. He was about twelve, maybe thirteen. The blond girl was riding in an overcrowded Mercedes 500 SL convertible with a bunch of other kids. The top was down and she sat up front, squashed in next to the driver. The driver was a fresh-faced senior who had probably just got his driver's license.

The group was obviously from Grandview. They were slumming around Creekside. They had ended up in a dark alley behind the Safeway on Dawson Street where the Cougars were busy breaking into the back of the store for cigarettes. The Mercedes' high beams caught them in the act like escapees in a searchlight beam.

Hulk had the wrecking bar. Mickey told him what to do, quietly in his ear so it wouldn't sound like an order. Hulk took his wrecking bar over to the throbbing Mercedes. Without breaking stride, he blinded its right eye with a well-aimed backhand swipe. Hulk didn't have a lot going for him between the ears, but he was a man of action, reacting like a caveman surprised by a roaring mastodon.

Hulk was about to do the same to the car's left eye but was stopped by the driver, Freshface, who leaped out of the car with a yell and stood between Hulk and the car headlight, his fists ready. Hulk hadn't expected anyone to challenge him. Hulk was way over six feet, weighed 180 pounds and had the wrecking bar. Freshface would be slaughtered. But Hulk's hesitation cost him the rest of the battle because the cute blond kid—she couldn't have been more than twelve or thirteen—stepped out of the car and stood between Hulk and Freshface.

Mickey could see she was scared. She said to Hulk, a quiver in her voice, "Go away and leave us alone."

Hulk just stood there with his mouth hanging open, puzzled. He was like King Kong the first time he ever saw the girl.

While Hulk was gaping, the girl grabbed Freshface and dragged him back into the car. The other four kids in the car were terrified. They just sat there saying nothing, their faces all shadows and fear.

Mickey had been standing back, behind Hulk. The rest of the gang, five of them that particular night, were hanging loose, grins on their faces, enjoying Hulk's embarrassment as the Mercedes roared off down the lane.

Afterward, Mickey thought about the nerve of that blond kid. Even though she was scared, she faced up to Hulk. Hulk in his black T-shirt with the sleeves torn off. Menacing her with muscles, tattoos and a thirty-inch wrecking bar! Plus the tough-looking-but-mostly-harmless Cougars behind him in the glare of that single headlight.

The blond kid hadn't noticed Mickey, of course. Back then he was only a skinny kid with a dirty face.

And now, here she was again. A couple of years older. She was looking into Mickey's eyes. She didn't know him.

But he recognized her all right. He'd never forget the way she'd stood there, the beam from the Mercedes back-lighting her hair, and Mickey feeling like a frog, awestruck at the sight of the beautiful princess.

Chapter Four

The band room was a quiet place. It was separated from the noise of the school by a long corridor and by its lonely basement location. Birgit's voice was low, her upper-crust tones casual. Mickey willed his eyes from her face and looked at Peter Miller lounging easily beside her.

"You both know Peter from the football team," said Birgit, smiling up at Peter.

They were a couple. It was obvious. Peter was an eleventh grader.

Peter smiled back at her like he owned her.

Freshface from years ago? Mickey wondered. No. Peter was only two years older than Mickey. Freshface, whoever he was, was graduated and long gone.

Peter was big and good-looking: blue eyes, expensively cut hair that flopped carelessly over onto his forehead. He wore sharp-looking jeans, cell phone clipped to the belt, white shirt, maroon sweater, Nike Airs. He and Birgit sat on the desk like a pair of matching bookends. He smiled. White, even teeth. "Hi, Michael," he said, following Birgit's lead.

It was the first time any member of the team had ever called Mickey by name—any name, Mickey or Michael.

Mickey nodded and lowered himself onto an old collapsed sofa beside Whisper. Whisper's real name was Winston Smith. He was a husky, thick-necked kid, almost as wide as he was tall. His face wore a permanent grin. Everyone on the football team called him Whisper because of his quiet, scratchy voice.

Whisper didn't seem to notice that Mickey was there. His eyes were locked on Birgit. "So tell us what we're doing here, baby," he asked her, grinning.

Except for two bottles of Snapple parked beside them on the desk, neither Birgit nor Peter appeared to have any lunch. They sat composed and unsmiling. They looked Mickey and Whisper over for several seconds without saying a word.

Mickey took a bite of his cheese-and-tomato sandwich and discovered he was no longer hungry. He dropped the sandwich back into the bag. He studied Birgit, comparing the girl he saw before him now with that gutsy kid who had faced up to Hulk that night in the alley. He had admired her then, and he admired her now. She was older now, of course, and more sure of herself. Her hair was shining and fine like silk. He waited for her to speak.

"I called this meeting," she said, "because you boys have something in common: you're football players and you're tough."

"Tough?" said Whisper.

Birgit smiled. "That's right, Whisper. I've watched you on the football field. You're like a bulldozer."

Birgit looked at Mickey. "You too, Michael. I heard you nailed one of the Agostino brothers Monday with your locker door. Too bad they ganged up on you. I hear that you're smart. And I've seen you play football. You play like it's a war."

Mickey said nothing. This was embarrassing. He was no tough guy. Everyone seemed to think that because you came from Creekside you were tough. And Birgit could tell by just looking at him that he wasn't one of them, that he was a Creekside kid.

Birgit turned to Peter. "And Peter is mean and tough when he needs to be."

Peter grinned, like a well-fed cat. Mickey half expected him to purr.

Whisper hadn't taken his eyes off Birgit. "We're tough. So what? Why are we here?"

"Before I answer that," said Birgit, "let me ask a question: Do you think this is a good school?"

Whisper cracked his knuckles. "It's okay, I guess."

"Michael?" Birgit uncrossed her legs.

Mickey shrugged. He was starting to discover that Grandview wasn't too much different from Creekside. He didn't say anything; Birgit had him tongue-tied.

Peter jumped in. "Grandview's a zoo! That's what I think!"

Whisper's grin disappeared for a moment while he nodded thoughtfully. "Peter's right, it's a friggin' zoo." He looked across at Mickey for the first time. "Ain't that the truth? A friggin' zoo?" Deep furrows in his worried brow.

Mickey shrugged again. He didn't like Whisper too much. The way he cracked his knuckles. The way he talked, like he was Tony Soprano.

"In what way is it a zoo?" Birgit asked Whisper.

"Well," Whisper said slowly, his grin reappearing, "this year there's more bullying going on; you see it every day.

Some of it's racial, but not all of it. Kids are getting mugged for their lunch money. Girls are just as bad. Sometimes they're worse. An eighth-grade girl was bullied into writing another kid's essay. Can you believe it?"

Peter cut in. "The terrorists are in charge. There are kids who've stopped coming to school because they're so scared of the bullies. My brother went to this school. It's changed since he was here. It used to be such a great place, but now they're letting all kinds of lowlife—" He stopped.

There was an uncomfortable silence for several seconds. Mickey knew just what the others were thinking. They were thinking of how there were no longer any school boundaries. They were thinking of how kids from places like Creekside were now allowed into Grandview. They were remembering that Mickey was from Creekside.

Whisper said to Birgit, "But I don't see how it's our problem. Why should we care? Do your time and then get out. That's what I say."

Birgit's face flushed pink. "You make it sound like a prison."

"That's what it is," said Whisper, cracking his knuckles.

"Grandview never used to be like this," said Birgit. "Why should we care, you ask? Well, I care because the animals are taking over. The low-class bullies are in charge. Why should we let them rule our lives?"

Whisper, without taking his eyes off Birgit, chomped his teeth into an apple.

Birgit looked at Mickey. "What do you think, Michael?"

He felt a squeeze under his heart. With her beautiful eyes on him he couldn't think of anything to say. It was like his brain had been vacuumed. All he could do was shrug his shoulders.

But she was right about the bullies. Last night he had tried to think of a way of getting back at those two fat slobs who bruised his ear, ribs and ego. And who stole his lunch. His ear still wasn't right.

"The school's a war zone, so what?" Whisper chipped in. He took his eyes off Birgit and glanced at his watch. He reached for his cell phone.

"Okay." Birgit's eyes flashed. "I'll tell you *so what*." She drew in a breath. Mickey watched her, mesmerized, unable to take his eyes from her face.

Whisper was also captivated by Birgit's fire. He returned the cell phone to his pocket.

"I called this meeting," said Birgit passionately, "because I want to do something about this zoo. I called this meeting because I want Grandview to be a normal, ordinary, decent school, the way it used to be. I called this meeting because I want to put the animals back in their cages, because I want the good people—like you and me—to win out over the bad people, the brutes and bullies. Good over evil. Brains over brutality. Class over trash. That's what I want. I called this meeting because I want you to help me. I want us to form a club, a society, a very special secret society that will help put an end to… to…to this terrible, mindless violence." She stopped, flushed and out of breath.

The three boys stared at her in stunned silence.

Chapter Five

"I want you to help me." Her words rang in his ears.

Mickey felt his heart twist in his chest. Birgit was dazzling. His mind disconnected from the band room. He traveled back in time to see again that pretty, spunky kid facing down a wrecking bar and Hulk's hundred-and-eighty pounds of mindless muscle.

Birgit was talking again, cooler now.

"My plan is to form a cleanup committee, a group to help put this place back together again. Mr. McCann can't do it." McCann was the school principal. "The teachers can't do it, so it's up to people like us. We could start by dealing with a few of the jerks, like the ones who beat up Joey Washington."

"I think it's a great idea," said Peter quietly. "It's about time something was done!" He paused. "And that's not all." He glanced quickly at Birgit. "I know a girl who was practically raped by three classmates—animals, more like—in the art supplies closet. She felt like she *had* been raped. I'm not kidding. They were girls, and they were suspended for—get this—*one day*! Can you believe it?" He was angry.

"You better believe it," said Birgit quietly. She looked at Mickey and Whisper. "The girl Peter's talking about

is me. They pinned me down and..."
She stopped, all choked up, and looked
down at her Reeboks.

Silence.

"So, what do you say?" said Peter.
"You guys ready to help put a stop
to it?"

"Put a stop to it?" said Whisper. "Are
you kidding? You've been watching too
many Bruce Willis videos, man. What
can the four of us do?"

Birgit's head snapped up.
"Punishment," she said.

"Punishment?" Whisper's smile
melted away.

"They must be punished," said Birgit
quietly. "And it will be a warning to
others. Word will get around. It will no
longer be the law of the jungle. It will
be law and order, decency and dignity."

"You're out of your mind," said
Whisper.

"No, I'm not. I know I'm right."

Whisper said, "So we're to be, what? A high school SWAT team? A hit squad?"

Birgit's chin lifted. "A hit squad maybe. But more like doctors. Let me tell you about…"

Mickey listened. He could sit and look and listen to Birgit all his life and never get bored.

"…my Uncle Helmut," Birgit continued. "He's a surgeon. When I was little I asked him how he cured people who had cancer. He told me he had to get the cancer early, before it spread through the whole body. All the diseased cells had to be cut out. None could be left. The body had to be purified and cleaned before the healing could start."

Nobody spoke.

Mickey could feel goose bumps on his arms.

"We need to be surgeons too," Birgit said. "We need to cut out Grandview's cancer." Her eyes moved from Peter to Whisper to Mickey and back to Peter. "It's up to smart, decent people like us to make things work properly. We don't need to wait until we're adults. We can start right now, here at Grandview High."

A long silence.

Whisper scratched his jaw and stared at Birgit. Mickey slumped farther down into the collapsed sofa and tried to free his eyes from her face but failed.

A pair of chattering kids opened the band room door, closed it and went away. Mickey could hear the sounds of kids clattering up and down the basement stairs. Whisper cracked his knuckles.

Birgit leaned back on the desk. She scrambled Mickey's brains by turning the full power of her eyes on him. Then she did the same to the others. She was in total command.

Peter said, "You can count me in, Birgit."

"Sure, why not?" croaked Whisper. "Count me in." He wasn't grinning now. Birgit's brilliance had dazzled him too, Mickey reckoned. Also, Whisper liked violence and brutality. Mickey had seen him on the field. It was never enough to tackle and bring another player down. He always had to add the extra sly punch. For Whisper, being in a hit squad would be fun. And being brutal for Birgit would be heaven.

Birgit smiled at Mickey. "Michael? Are you in?"

Of course he was in. Why wouldn't he be in? Birgit was a knockout. He would do anything for her. And wouldn't it be great to hit Birgit's "animals"?

And the Agostino brothers? And hadn't he been waiting a long time for an invitation to Grandview society? You bet he was in.

But he didn't want to seem too eager. He had to play it cool.

"Sure." He shrugged. "I'm in."

chapter six

Mickey rolled his old Carlton racer home down the hill in a daze.

Headlines: Mickey Cord Meets Amazingly Beautiful Girl. Astonishingly Rich and Beautiful Girl Falls for Poor but Honest Creekside Kid.

But he was fooling himself. Birgit wasn't for him; she was too much, too unattainable. And she had Purring Peter.

And anyway, a girl with a surgeon-uncle named after a Viking was simply too much for a kid named after a mouse.

And Mickey didn't think he was as tough or as smart as Birgit thought he was. He was smarter than Heck maybe—who used to be called Hulk— but that wasn't saying much.

He came to a stop in the driveway of Hobbit House. He parked his bike in the shed. Hobbit House was a big old three-story building with cedar shakes and an open front porch.

The shed was full of junk. Mickey's bike was saved from being junk because even though it was an old, beat-up racer he took good care of it. He oiled it every weekend and dismantled and greased the bottom bracket and oiled the chain every couple of weeks or so.

Heck was in the living room, sprawled out on the ragged sofa, watching cartoons on TV with Sammy and Jimmy. The kids treated Heck like a slightly younger brother. Mickey tried to sneak up the stairs, but Heck heard him and leaped to his feet. He was overjoyed to see Mickey, as usual. If he had a tail it would've been wagging.

"Hey, Mickey!"

"Hi, Heck," Mickey said over his shoulder as Heck followed him up to their room. Mickey didn't call him Hulk anymore. The Hobbits said it wasn't a nice name and he should be called by his proper name, Hector. The other kids in the home argued that Hector was a dumb name, so they called him Heck, a compromise.

Heck was supposed to be out looking for work. He should have left Hobbit House a couple of years ago, when he was eighteen. That was when the government stopped paying his bills.

But the Hobbits let him keep his old room—it was Mickey's now too—when he was released from the minimum-security prison. The Hobbits had been keeping him ever since. Which was real nice of them, Mickey thought, because they weren't getting a penny from the government.

Larry and Annie Hobbs, the Hobbits, ran the group home. They were from England originally. Mickey didn't know who in the distant past started calling it Hobbit House, but the name stuck. The Hobbits were okay. Mickey had lived in some pretty awful places, but he struck it lucky the day he got sent to Hobbit House. That was about four years ago.

Larry Hobbs was a big, serious man, built like a marble monument, with gray hair. An ex-policeman, he now worked days downtown in the courthouse as a security guard. Most of the time he looked like he was angry about something. Usually his big face crumpled into a frown and his bottom lip pushed out and he would start growling at some country for bombing some other country. Or at the government for promising stuff and then going back on its word. Or at the way people in Africa were being allowed to die of AIDS. Larry reading the *Vancouver Sun* was a kettle coming slowly to the boil. But his anger was never at anyone or anything in the house. He never even got mad at Heck, and Heck was an adult who never looked for work. But Larry never blamed Heck. "You can only play the hand you're dealt," he always said.

His wife, Annie Hobbs, didn't say much. Annie had long brown hair with a gray streak in it, usually worn in a braid, and her eyes were a pale watery blue. She was a pretty good cook. She was easygoing, never hassled anyone except Larry. She cooked and cleaned and never complained except for telling Larry to cancel his newspaper subscription before he had a heart attack.

The other kids in the house were Sammy, eleven; Jimmy, twelve; and Candy, thirteen. Candy was the only girl. Sammy and Jimmy were nice ordinary kids who shared a room and went to Creekside Elementary. They stayed out of trouble, mainly because Larry and Annie kept a watchful eye on them.

Candy, however, refused to go to school. She was supposed to be in the eighth grade. She had a big fight about it with Larry a year ago, when she first came to Hobbit House. "I can educate myself," she told him. "I don't need no school to tell *me* what to do."

She borrowed books from the library and read them in the tiny room she had all to herself. Larry accepted Candy's decision not to go to school and defended her against the school inspector. "Is this a free country or what?" he argued.

Candy was nice to everyone, but she was especially nice to Heck. "He can't help the way he is," she said. This echoed Larry's point of view. Candy watched over Heck like she was his mother.

Mickey threw himself onto his bed. Heck sat on the edge of his own bed, asking Mickey questions. He often did that. But all Mickey wanted was to be alone so he could think about the meeting in the band room and about Birgit Neilsen.

"Hey, Mickey, what do you say?" Grinning, specks of saliva at the corner of his mouth, eager like a puppy.

"I've got nothing to say, Heck. I'm bushed. Leave me alone, will you?"

"Look, Mickey! I mended my jeans, see? It's an iron patch, that's what Annie said it is, an iron patch. She showed me how to do it, see?"

"Didn't you hear me? I said leave me alone!"

His face fell. "Leave you alone?"

"You heard me right."

The excitement went out of Heck's face. He stared at Mickey dumbly, then turned away and shuffled out of the room. Mickey could hear him clumping down the stairs, back to the kids and the TV.

Mickey felt like a rat.

Supper that night was fish burgers and salad. Larry always sat at the head of the table, opposite Annie. Annie kept jumping up and down as she hustled back and forth between table and kitchen. Heck and Mickey sat on one side, as usual, and Candy and Sammy and Jimmy sat on the other. It was a long table, with room for a couple more people. Mickey had seen a time when all the chairs were full, but right now there were only the five kids, if you could call Heck a kid, though he sure acted like one.

Larry waved his fork and ranted on about how big corporations paid hardly any taxes. Except for Candy, none of the others were really interested in that kind of stuff. Not even Annie. But Candy always seemed interested in what was going on. When Larry paused to catch his breath, Candy usually jumped in with a whole bunch of questions.

Mickey looked across at her while she and Larry carried on with their discussion. Candy was no Birgit Neilsen, but she was okay. She was an ordinary girl, skinny, all sharp angles, brown eyes and mop of dark hair. He tried to tune them all out as they chattered together like birds. He thought about the secret meeting. Heck helped himself to more salad from the bowl. Annie sat smiling and watching. Candy was saying something, trying to catch Mickey's attention, but he didn't notice. He was too busy thinking about Birgit Neilsen.

Chapter Seven

He thought about her all weekend.

Candy noticed. "Have you got something on your mind, Mickey?" she asked him on Sunday morning.

Heck was out front, shooting baskets with Sammy and Jimmy.

Mickey shook his head.

"Do you want to come with me and Heck to church?"

"No thanks."

"Heck would like it if you did. You know how much he loves being in church. With the singing and all. And everyone dressed up. It's the only time he gets to wear his jacket and tie and his good black shoes."

"No thanks."

"He thinks an awful lot of you, Mickey. You know that, don't you? He looks up to you."

"I hear Joey Washington's out of hospital. I thought I'd go see how he is."

"You could see Joey after church."

"No thanks."

Candy looked at him. Those brown eyes of hers had a way of looking at him sometimes like she was reading his mind. She smiled. She had a nice smile. The corner of her mouth tilted up on one side slightly more than the other. It was a tilted kind of smile. But it made sense

because she was a tilted kind of girl.
"Suit yourself," she said.

He biked over to Joey's Creekside house where he lived with three brothers and two sisters. His mom and dad had taken the other kids to church. Joey was home alone. He was wearing dark glasses. His face was swollen and discolored below the glasses. He let Mickey in, moving slowly as if he was in pain. He switched off the TV and then lay on the couch, moving carefully. His right arm was in a sling.

"So how are you feeling, Joey?" said Mickey. "What's with the sling?"

Talking was difficult for Joey. He spoke slowly. "Broken collarbone. Broken rib. Black eyes. Split lip."

"School washroom, right?"

"Right. Two big guys. They jumped me soon as I came through the door."

"They take anything? Money?"

"Nothing. Didn't even go through my pockets. Just kicked the crap out of me and told me to go back to Creekside."

Mickey didn't stay long. Joey was finding it hard to talk.

On Monday the secret society met again. Birgit sat on the desk, same as before. She said, "We need a name for our secret society. Any suggestions?"

"Hit Squad," Whisper whispered.

"Okay," said Birgit. "But it sounds a bit much, don't you think? A bit heavy? How about Grandview Cleanup Committee?" She looked around. "Any other suggestions? Peter? Michael?"

Peter said, "I like your suggestion, Birgit. Cleanup Committee sounds good." Today he sat on the sofa beside Whisper. Mickey was beginning to dislike Peter, the way he always sucked up to Birgit. Mickey sat in the over-stuffed chair.

Birgit looked amazing in skirt and kneesocks. Whisper wore good stuff too. Mickey hadn't noticed on Friday. Today he had on a plain white cotton T-shirt, a lambskin leather jacket and fitted jeans that molded to his big thighs. Mickey was the odd man out: same old jeans, wearing thin at the knees; gray Value Village nylon jacket; blue Army & Navy sports shirt, one of three he rotated; collapsed no-name runners.

"Let's take a vote," said Birgit. "Who's for Grandview Cleanup Committee?" She put up her own hand. Peter's followed.

Birgit said, "Hit Squad?"

Whisper and Mickey put up their hands.

"A tie," said Birgit.

Peter held up a coin. "Heads for Cleanup; tails for Hit Squad." He tossed it in the air.

"Hit Squad it is then," said Birgit. "Next item on the agenda: we've got to swear an oath of secrecy. Nobody knows who we are or what we do. Agreed?"

The three boys nodded.

Birgit said, "We must swear never to tell. Hold up your right hands and say, 'I swear!'"

The three boys held up their hands. "I swear!" they said.

"That nobody knows who we are or what we do," said Birgit.

"That nobody knows who we are or what we do," they repeated.

"Okay, let's get to it," said Birgit. "Our first cleanup job, I mean hit. I say let's get the thugs who beat up Joey Washington. He's out of hospital but he was hurt pretty bad. The only reason he was mugged was because of his skin color. It's obvious. They didn't try to steal from him. Can you believe it? Any other suggestions?"

Whisper whispered to Mickey, "What skin color is this guy?"

Mickey whispered back, "Black."

Peter said, "What about the three animals who assaulted you in the stockroom?"

Birgit's eyes gleamed. "If you like. I just didn't want it to be only *my* agenda. Any other suggestions?"

Mickey almost suggested the Agostino brothers, but he held back. There was lots of time to get those slobs.

Silence.

Then Whisper spoke. "I heard what they did to you. They're scum. We can take care of Joey's muggers later. When we find out who they are."

"Let's hit Birgit's attackers, the three animals," said Peter, nodding.

"Michael?" said Birgit.

"Fine by me," he said.

"The three animals it is," said Birgit. "Shelley Crewell. Jessie Jones. Mona Teasedale. Our first hit."

Chapter Eight

Mona Teasedale didn't know why she'd felt so bad all day.

She wondered whether she should call Shelley and Jessie and say she was sick. But she would miss the party tonight at Red Grinwald's. Red was nineteen and shared an apartment with Tommy Garr, also nineteen. Mona usually had a good time at Red's.

He never seemed to mind if you didn't bring any booze or grass; he always had lots. So she was reluctant to stay home. Maybe she'd feel better once she got out of her boring house where all her mother ever did was watch TV. Her dad had split years ago.

Two hours later, at the party, she still felt wobbly. Red's apartment was wall-to-wall people, and the music thumped in time with her headache. She saw Red's pig-shaved head coming at her through the crowd.

"Take a shot of this, Mona baby, and you'll feel great." He held out a glass.

She'd already had too much beer. "No thanks, Red. I think I'd better find the others and go home."

He put the glass down on a table and reached his hands around to massage the back of her neck. The skin of his fingers was rough from his bricklaying. He had a brick-red complexion too.

And his hair used to be red before he shaved it all off.

"Come and lie down for a while."

Mona could see Red's bedroom from where she stood. "No thanks, Red." She spotted Shell across the room with Tommy. They were necking.

"I'll give you a massage. You'll feel better." Red had to shout over the noise of the music video.

"I said good night, Red." She crossed the floor and yelled in her friend's ear. "Shell, get Jessie. I've gotta go. I don't feel good, okay? You coming or do you want to stay?"

Shelley pouted. She didn't relish the thought of walking home alone, but she wanted to stay. "Can you take me home later, Tommy?"

Tommy shook his head. "Can't drive." He grinned. "License suspended. Why don't you stay, Shell, we got room." He grinned again.

Shelley shook her head. "Okay, Mona, I'm coming. I'll grab Jessie. Good night, Tommy. Maybe another time."

When the three girls got outside it was cold and dark. It had been raining. Streetlights reflected off the slick pavement. Mona felt lousy. She couldn't wait to get into bed. Shelley and Jessie were talking nonstop, but the words just flew over Mona's aching head.

They turned the corner onto Pandora Street where it was darker and the wind cut into Mona's ribs. She thrust her fists deep into her pockets.

A van screeched to a stop right across their path and three black-clothed figures leaped out from the front. Their faces were hidden behind ski masks. The girls screamed. Mona felt herself thrust violently into the back of the van with her two friends. The three girls fell in a heap together, yelling and struggling, on the van floor. Two of the attackers jumped in behind them and slammed the door shut.

The van took off, tires squealing. Mona struggled to a sitting position, heart beating so fast she was sure it was about to burst. She fought to get her breath. They were being kidnapped. She tried to keep her head as she felt another wave of panic sweep over her. She must think. There were four of them— two in back, two in front. The two in front just looked straight ahead out the windshield.

Mona looked out the window. They were heading toward downtown. Whenever they reached a lighted area, Mona saw that Shelley's and Jessie's faces were white with fear.

What did they want? It couldn't be a kidnap for money. The next thought to flash into her head was so frightening it made her lash out with her bare fists at the closest kidnapper, who fell back into the driver. The car swerved dangerously. One of the men in the back grabbed her arms and pulled her away while the other slapped her face. The blow stung. Mona started to cry.

"What do you want? Where are you taking us?" demanded Shelley fiercely.

Now that Mona had recovered a little from her initial shock she had time to look at their captors more closely. They were built like high school kids. Could they be from Grandview?

They had driven through downtown. Now they were headed down Georgia Street, toward Stanley Park.

Soon they were in the park, the twin beams of the van's headlights picking out tall stands of cedar and pine in the dark mist.

Mona was scared. There was no way they'd be able to run for it here. Where could they run? The park was so big.

Shelley groaned and muttered something Mona couldn't hear.

The van lurched to a stop. The doors were thrown open. The three ninth-grade girls were dragged out roughly onto the grass. Mona was trembling. The ski masks gave the four kidnappers an even more menacing appearance in this dark and deserted place. One of them forced her over to the front of the van and into the glare of its headlights. He pulled her wrists around and behind a tree and tied them together. He was very rough. She could tell he was enjoying her pain and terror. He was laughing quietly, a low whisper of a laugh. He had tied her wrists too tight. The pain made her bite her lip. She could hear Shelley and Jessie yelling behind her. She turned, crab-like, around the tree trunk until she could see her friends. They were also tied to trees. They were terrified.

One of the kidnappers was carrying something from the van, a loaded pack-sack it looked like. Mona squinted but couldn't see properly because of the blinding headlights.

The kidnappers did not speak. Mona thought they had to be from Grandview High. Where else? The whole thing had been planned, but why? What was this all about? Who at Grandview would do a thing like this? Was it Bobbie Agostino? He was cruel enough. He'd asked her out and she had turned him down in front of his brother and a bunch of his friends. Not only that but she had laughed and called him a sicko. Told him she didn't go out with perverts. It was stupid of her, she knew. But she couldn't resist insulting the guy. He was such a loser. This kidnapping caper was just the kind of thing he'd think up. But why drag Shelley and Jessie into it? Because they just happened to be there? That didn't make sense. Then she thought of that Neilsen girl. Birgit! The one they got down on the art stockroom floor. Shelley and Jessie were in on that one. The three of them were.

Mona felt sick, and it wasn't because of all the booze she had drunk at Red's. She looked over at Shelley and Jessie. They looked sick too. Maybe the same suspicion was going through their heads. That the blond girl was the one behind it. If it really was Birgit Neilsen, what could they do? Tell the police? Mona hated the police. Tell the school principal, Mr. McCann? Forget it. Complaining to the principal would get them nowhere. Besides, how could they prove it was Birgit?

Shelley spoke up, yelling, in a panic. "Don't you know kidnapping is a federal offense?" She had heard that line in a dozen movies.

There was no answer. So far, except for that whispery laugh, the kidnappers had remained silent.

Mona wanted to throw up; she was going to pass out. Her legs wouldn't support her properly. The pain in her wrists was unbearable. She slumped against the tree and slid down to its base. Her aching arms were stretched behind her. She sat on the cold wet ground. Her hair was grabbed roughly from behind. She heard the sound of scissors. Her hair was being lopped off in hunks!

Mona cried. She couldn't bear to think of her beautiful hair being cut off. What would she tell everybody, especially her mother? She couldn't see her two friends now. Her head was being held back and all she could see was the canopy of tree branches above. The scissors had stopped. Now she could feel her head being painted with a wide brush.

And then her hands were free. She felt her head with her fingertips. Her fingers had very little feeling left in them. Hardly anything was left of her hair under the sticky wet paint. She wiped away her tears with the backs of her wrists. She could hear her friends sobbing.

"Shell!" she cried. "Jessie!"

The kidnappers were in their van. Mona could not see the license plate number. She heard the doors slam shut and the motor start. The light and sound receded as the van drove away, and she was left in darkness. "Shell?" she cried. "Jess?"

Chapter Nine

"It was so sweet!" said Whisper, cracking a knuckle for extra emphasis.

Monday in the band room. Peter was on the broken-spring couch beside Whisper where he could keep his eyes on Birgit. Mickey was sitting in the easy chair. Birgit was in her usual place high on the desk, smiling down on them.

"And so easy," said Peter with a laugh.

"And so thrilling!" said Birgit, excited. "I haven't done anything that wild and...*satisfying* in my whole life! I loved it! I doubt if those three pigs will show their faces for a month. It will take at least a week to get all the yellow paint off their heads."

Birgit turned to Mickey. "What do you say, Michael?"

Mickey nodded. He hadn't taken his eyes off Birgit since he'd first walked in. None of the boys had. "The hit went just the way we planned," he said. "Stealing the van, grabbing the girls, everything." It was the most he'd ever said to her.

"But did you enjoy it?" said Birgit.

"Yeah. It was okay," Mickey admitted. He really wasn't so sure. It was fun working with Birgit and the two boys. They were a good team.

And it made him feel a part of the Grandview crowd. But there was something about the whole operation he hadn't enjoyed. Every time he tried to figure out what it was, his brain short-circuited, wanting to think of Birgit instead.

"The important thing is," said Birgit, "that the word will get around. It will be a wake-up call for all the other lowlife bullies at Grandview."

Whisper cracked his knuckles. "So who's next?"

"Joey Washington's muggers," said Birgit. "Agreed?"

The boys nodded.

Birgit turned to Mickey. "You talked to Joey, Michael. Does he know who these scumbags are?"

"Only one. Guy named Gordie Tweed," said Mickey. "He didn't know the name of the other one. But they're a pair. They go everywhere together.

They pick on Asian kids and gays. Shouldn't be difficult to find out the second name."

Birgit smiled. "Gordie Tweed. I know that creep. Tenth grader. Let's find out who his psycho friend is. We meet here Friday lunch hour. Okay?"

"Gino Bibby. He's our number two man," said Whisper, cracking his knuckles.

Mickey said, "I had Joey ID Tweed and Bibby, just to make sure we get the right guys."

Birgit said, "Joey's back at school?"

Mickey nodded. "Got bored watching TV."

Whisper continued quietly, "Bibby and Tweed won't be easy to take down. They're big and they're tough. They work out four or five hours a day at the gym. They're bodybuilders."

Peter said, "So what are you saying? We need more muscle?"

"Not if we take them one at a time," said Mickey.

Peter boasted, "I know them and I know we can handle them. No problem. There are only two of them and four of us. Three, not counting Birgit." He smiled winningly at her. "We don't want to see Birgit get hurt."

Mickey cringed inwardly. Peter was beginning to have a painful effect on him.

"If we try to take them together, three bodies won't be enough," said Whisper. "We need at least four."

"I've got a friend who can help us out," said Mickey. "Why don't you leave the muscle problem to me?"

Chapter Ten

Heck liked to take a turn at kitchen cleanup after supper, but he only got in the way. Or he broke something in his ham-sized fists.

The kids were watching TV; the Hobbits were reading.

It was Mickey and Candy's turn for the dishes. Mickey dried and Candy washed. Heck came in, filling the

kitchen with his bulk. Mickey usually
left it to Candy to get rid of him. She
knew how to do it nicely so his feelings
weren't hurt.

As soon as Heck had gone off to join
the kids in front of the TV, Candy was
angry. "I can't believe what I'm hearing,
Mickey. Tell me it's not true."

Mickey's heart sank. Play the innocent, he thought. "What's not true,
Candy?"

"You asked Heck to help out in some
funny business. He won't tell me what.
Says it's a secret. I'm warning you,
Mickey, if you get Heck into any kind
of trouble, you'll have the Hobbits to
answer to. And me."

Her eyes flashed. Candy was really
something when she was mad. Wild hair,
flashing brown eyes, pink cheeks. That
was the trouble with Heck: he couldn't
keep his big mouth shut. Well, at least he
hadn't told Candy anything more.

"It's nothing to get upset about, Candy, just a harmless little caper. One evening's work, that's all."

"Tell me what you're up to. I don't want Heck mixed up in something illegal. If he goes to jail again, it'll be for serious time."

"Candy, I told you. It's nothing."

"Okay. I'll tell the Hobbits and they'll ground him for the next month. He won't even be allowed into the backyard."

Mickey groaned. "Aw, come on. There's no need—"

"So tell me what it's all about."

"I can't tell. I took an oath of secrecy."

"You're kidding!"

"It's true."

Candy thought for a few seconds; then she said, "You're allowed to break an oath for one minute if it's for someone's good. But you have to circle the room three times widdershins."

"You're making that up. I don't believe you." Mickey looked at her to see if she was serious. She was. She was Irish. Her parents were killed in a car crash. They had that in common. Mickey's parents were also killed in a car crash when he was only seven. He'd been in foster homes ever since. The Hobbits' was his fourth. And his last, he hoped.

"What's widdershins?"

"You circle to your left." She pointed a handful of knives and forks at the kitchen floor. "Do it."

Mickey did it. He walked three times in a circle around the kitchen. Then he told Candy about the girls who attacked Birgit and what the Hit Squad did to them.

"What's this got to do with Heck?"

Mickey said, "If you bothered to go to school, I wouldn't have to explain all this."

He told her about Joey Washington. Candy listened without interruption.

"So we need Heck as backup muscle. These guys are big and mean. Look, the minute's up. I can't tell you anything else."

"What do you plan to do to these guys? Cut off their hair and paint their heads, same as those poor girls?"

Mickey shrugged. "Probably. It's not all figured out yet. Why are you being so sarcastic?"

Candy frowned as she let the last pot drop with a clatter onto the drain board. "Sounds to me like you really enjoyed doing it to those girls, cutting off their hair and everything. You enjoyed it, Mickey, didn't you?"

Mickey shrugged. "I don't know."

"Gave you a feeling of power, right? You enjoyed making those girls suffer." Candy's eyes glittered like pins.

"They were pigs. Bullies. They had it coming."

Candy grabbed a towel and helped with the last of the drying. She said nothing and wouldn't meet his eye.

After a while he couldn't stand her silence.

"What?"

She said nothing.

Louder. "What?"

She gave a sniff. "Well." She stopped. "I don't see much difference between you and the bad guys. Seems to me your so-called Hit Squad is just as bad as the bullies you're out to get."

Chapter Eleven

Mickey usually ate alone in the school cafeteria, but today Peter and Whisper joined him. They discussed the hit on Tweed and Bibby, Joey Washington's attackers.

"Keep your voices down," warned Whisper.

Mickey felt good that he now had Grandview friends. He'd noticed in the

last few days that other members of
the football team were starting to
give him friendly smiles and nods and
call him by name. "Hi there, Michael,"
they said. Had Whisper or Peter been
telling other football players about
the hit on the three girls? If not, why
had they become so friendly all of a
sudden? What about that oath of
secrecy? He remembered talking to
Candy. She had sure fooled him with
that widdershins garbage. But was he
really fooled? Or had he just used it
as an excuse to talk about something
that had been worrying him? Used it
as an opportunity to get something off
his chest?

But he had broken Birgit's secrecy
oath, he knew that. And this made him
feel bad too.

Then Mickey saw something that
made him feel sick. He gave Whisper

and Peter a nudge and pointed. Over on the other side of the cafeteria their two future victims, Tweed and Bibby, were giving Billy Rudge a hard time.

Everyone knew Billy Rudge. Billy was mentally challenged. Everyone liked him because of his constant smile and his eagerness to please. He cleaned and waited tables during the lunch hour and was paid a free lunch. He was wearing his Canucks T-shirt and backward baseball cap.

Tweed and Bibby had Billy running back and forth as he did his best to try and please them. When Billy brought their order, Tweed sent him back. "That ain't it, Billy! I asked for a Coke, not a 7UP. And bring a bag of chips, the vinegar kind!"

"Hey! Billy! I didn't order a ham sandwich; I ordered tuna on rye," yelled Bibby rudely.

"Billy, I changed my mind," said Tweed. "Forget the chips and bring me a burger. No onions, lots of ketchup. You got that?"

Billy looked miserable as he tried to remember the orders. When he thought he had it all figured out he gave a triumphant grin. "I'll be quick as I can, guys," he stammered and ran off to the kitchen. As he ran past, Bibby and Tweed stuck out their legs to trip him. Billy stumbled and almost fell.

The other kids in the area, some of them seniors, failed to come to Billy's aid. Instead they looked away, afraid of the two bullies.

Whisper grinned and cracked his knuckles. "Teaching those two creeps some manners is going to be a real pleasure."

Peter agreed. "You can say that again."

They watched the comings and goings of Gordie Tweed and Gino Bibby for a whole week. Then, when they thought they had enough information on their daily routines, they struck.

Chapter Twelve

Saturday afternoon. Mickey, Peter and Heck hung around the parking lot in front of the Oakridge Theatres, waiting for a large vehicle to show up, a van preferably, something old and easy to steal.

It wasn't long before a VW van parked. A father and three kids got out and headed for *The Lord of the Rings* matinee. They waited until the father and kids had disappeared inside the cinema. Then they stole their van. Mickey wired the ignition. Peter did the driving. He was a good driver. Plenty of experience. Peter didn't mind everyone knowing he owned a new Lexus.

The Lord of the Rings was a long movie. It guaranteed them a few hours before the van was reported stolen.

They picked up Birgit and Whisper and their bags of ski masks and baseball bats.

No scissors this time, just the bats.

They discussed the van seating. There was plenty of room. Then they drove over to the Hastings Pool Hall. Peter parked the van on the opposite side of the street. They waited.

Mickey introduced Heck to the others.

"Hi, Heck," said Birgit and Peter together.

"Glad to have you along, Heck," said Whisper.

"Have I seen you someplace before?" asked Birgit.

"I dunno," said Heck happily.

The wait wasn't long. They watched Tweed and Bibby leave the pool hall and climb into Tweed's old Pontiac. The Pontiac started with a roar and headed up the street belching thick clouds of exhaust smoke.

Peter followed. Soon they were in thickening city traffic, on Cambie, heading toward downtown. When they reached Broadway, the Pontiac darted over into the right lane and turned right. Peter followed. The Pontiac turned right onto Yukon and sped up the hill to 12th, then sharp right and over to Cambie again, completing a circle.

"They're onto us," said Peter. "They know they're being followed.

The Pontiac ran a red light at Broadway. Peter braked to a stop.

"I lost them!" Peter pounded the wheel in frustration.

When the light changed, Peter pushed his foot to the floor. They raced over Cambie Bridge. As they flew down the off-ramp at Seymour, the Pontiac was once again in sight, heading for the waterfront.

"Good work, Peter," said Birgit.

They chased through downtown streets, taking chances at the lights.

They followed the Pontiac into Gastown, the oldest part of the city. Water Street was crowded with people. The Pontiac stopped at a crosswalk to let the tourists cross.

"We've got them!" said Birgit.

Peter caught up behind the Pontiac, still stuck at the crossing.

Tweed and Bibby jumped out of their car and made a run for it through the crowds.

"Let's go!" said Whisper. They all leaped out of the van. Mickey, Peter and Whisper had baseball bats. Heck didn't need one.

"What about the ski masks?" said Peter.

"Never mind them. Just go!" yelled Birgit.

They ran, pushing their way through the thick crowds of shoppers and sightseers. Mickey felt the thrill of the chase. It was like those pictures in the British magazines. The hounds were running the foxes to earth. The quarry was in sight, running scared.

It wouldn't be long now. Soon Joey Washington would be revenged.

Chapter Thirteen

Mickey spotted Tweed and Bibby running past Gassy Jack's statue. But then the pair suddenly disappeared.

Birgit yelled, "Did you see where they went?"

"Must've ducked in somewhere." Peter was panting.

"Quick! In here," Whisper growled.

They followed him in through the back door of a spaghetti restaurant. Then they ran down several flights of steps into a dim and dirty basement. It was unlighted except for what daylight could filter down through metal grills in the sidewalk above.

Mickey knew where they were: it was the old area of the city, rebuilt after the fire of 1886. He remembered it from an elementary school field trip. The fire had burned down several blocks. The builders of the new city had raised the streets high above the old sidewalks. What remained of the original city was now a dark wasteland of deserted tunnels. In many places, light and water forced their way in through chinks in the brickwork and concrete. The hollow tunnels slept in silent gloom for block after block. It was a dank, stale-smelling, empty underworld. The few outside doors that led down to the tunnels were secured with heavy padlocks. There were, however, ways through to the underground city by means of the old basement steps of a few Gastown shops and hotels. It was through one of these that they now made their way. There were several signs saying *Keep Out* and *No Trespassing*.

Mickey shivered. The place was scary. He stumbled forward over the uneven floor.

Whisper led the way. He stopped in the semidarkness. He warned the others to be quiet. They listened. Mickey could hear running, scrambling sounds echoing back at them through the vaulted chambers. It was Tweed and Bibby ahead of them, trying to escape.

Whisper rasped, "Come on!"

A sudden noise made them all jump. Mickey looked up in fright. They had disturbed a flock of pigeons up on the thick beams.

They moved as quickly as they could in the musty belly of the old city, following the echoing sounds ahead. They passed faded storefronts, almost 120 years old, and peered into their dusty innards. Mickey felt the presence of gray ghosts, the spirits of men and women long fled from the wood floors and high counters. Water dripped through in places and rotted the wood. Or it gathered in pools to trickle off along the uneven ground to lower levels and disappear.

Mickey suddenly had the strangest feeling: he felt as though they had all been transported to another place in another time. This place under the streets of the city was a fantasy world. There was nothing real here. The laws of human behavior did not apply in this place because it was a place of the dead. He felt as though they had stumbled through a curtain of time into another dimension.

"I don't like it here, Mickey," whispered Heck nervously. "Could we go home now?"

"Relax, Heck," said Mickey as they passed a roped-off area. A painted sign, *Danger. Keep Out,* barred its entrance.

"Dead end," said Peter. The sound of shoes on crumbling plaster came from inside what was once a hotel. Whisper led the way into one of its doorless openings. The farther in they went, the dimmer it became.

Suddenly Tweed and Bibby appeared. They rushed out of the darkness and fled back out into the roped-off area.

"After them!" yelled Birgit.

They ran as hard as they dared over the uneven terrain, Mickey urging the slower Heck along. They caught up with Tweed and Bibby at yet another barrier with boards and ropes and a sign reading *Danger* in red paint.

"We've got 'em!" Whisper panted. Tweed and Bibby, their eyes wild, chests heaving, were trying to decide whether to risk going over the barrier. Ahead of them, behind the ropes, a flight of steps descended to another level with more red-painted signs: *Danger. Do Not Enter*.

Tweed and Bibby were trapped.

The Squad advanced on them, three with baseball bats.

"Let them have it!" yelled Birgit. A thin mustache of sweat beaded her upper lip.

Mickey moved forward with the others, baseball bat at the ready. In the danger area behind the barrier he could now see that part of the old street, at some time in the recent past, had collapsed in the center, leaving only narrow wooden beams, or catwalks, on the sides.

Tweed and Bibby ran from the baseball bats. They leaped over the rope barrier and started over one of the narrow catwalks, aiming to reach safety on the opposite side of the collapsed street. Whisper started to move forward in pursuit but Birgit yelled, "Stop! It's too risky. Let them go."

But it was too late for Heck to change his mental gears; he was already lumbering after the two muggers onto the catwalk.

Then everything happened at once. Tweed and Bibby came to a halt in the middle of the catwalk. Heck caught up with them. Their combined weight caused the beam to sag. There was a loud crack of splintering timber and the sound of falling masonry.

Mickey's stomach flipped. "Come back, Heck!" he yelled.

But the three boys were frozen to the spot.

"Run for it, Heck," screamed Mickey.

But Heck was too terrified to move.

Mickey would have to go out there and bring him back. He started forward with a rush.

"Stop him!" cried Birgit.

Mickey hadn't gone two yards before Whisper tackled him.

"Hang on to him," Birgit yelled.

Mickey tried to free himself but Whisper's arms were clamped around his legs.

Birgit stooped and yelled in Mickey's ear. "You go out there, Michael, and you're toast!"

"But Heck…"

"Let him go," she yelled. "He's just a big nobody. He's not one of us!"

Crack! A sound like a rifle shot. It was the beam collapsing.

Whisper fell back, releasing Mickey. They watched in horror. The underground cavern exploded with the roar of falling timber and masonry.

When the noise stopped, Mickey looked down into the crater. He could see nothing because of the thick gray dust that hung in the half darkness.

Whisper and Peter stood frozen with horror. Birgit was in shock. She stood staring at the empty place beyond the rope, the knuckles of both fists pressed to her trembling mouth.

Mickey ran back the way they had come, followed by the others. He found the stairs down to the next level.

"I'll go call for an ambulance," yelled Peter, heading up the stairs toward the street.

Mickey threw himself down the stairs. Birgit and Whisper followed. They ran back along the lower level to the site of the collapse. Through the swirling dust clouds Mickey could see the outlines of the beam and the pile of masonry and plaster where Heck had disappeared.

Whisper grabbed his arm. "It's not safe, Mickey!" he croaked. "You could get hurt!"

"I've got to find Heck!" Mickey strained to escape Whisper's grip on his arm.

"Wait!" Birgit shouted. "Wait until the dust clears."

Mickey couldn't wait. He pulled himself free. He had to find Heck. He felt his way forward through the dusty air. Birgit and Whisper followed cautiously, coughing.

"Heck!" Mickey shouted.

"Over here!" came a cry.

It was Bibby, pinned under a mound of brick and timber. Whisper and Birgit began moving masonry and debris to free him. Mickey continued his search. "Heck?" he yelled.

"Arrgh!"

It was Tweed, covered in dust and plaster. He had been thrown aside and was lying against the shattered beam, unable to stand because of his legs. "I think they're broken," he moaned.

"Help's on the way." Mickey left him. He'd survive. "Heck!" he yelled again.

And then he saw him. Heck's head and shoulders. The rest of him was pinned under the beam. He was quite still, his eyes closed.

Mickey climbed over the debris and crouched. He placed his fingers at Heck's throat, feeling for a pulse.

Nothing. He wiped dust and sweat from his face with the back of his hand and tried again. It was no good. Heck was gone.

Chapter Fourteen

Supper was spicy black beans and feta cheese with Mexican tomato salad. It was good, but Mickey wasn't hungry; he couldn't eat.

Nobody had spoken for several minutes.

It was the day after the accident.

Yesterday, the police had questioned him for an hour at police headquarters.

And the others, of course, Birgit, Peter and Whisper. They were questioned separately. All the parents had to be there. Mickey had Larry, who had just finished work. The others had their doctor and lawyer parents. The police let Mickey go. They said they were still investigating the incident and that charges might follow. Mickey hoped there would be charges. A spell in jail was exactly what he needed.

Then when he got home there had been a hundred more questions. Now they were finished. Now there was silence.

Mickey couldn't help noticing the glances everyone gave Heck's empty chair, especially young Sammy and Jimmy. The vacant space was like a gap in a fence.

Mickey asked Candy for the salt but she didn't seem to hear him. She hadn't looked at him since he got back from the police station. And she had taken no part in the question-and-answer session either. She looked numb.

Annie leaned over and passed Mickey the salt.

"Why doesn't someone say something?" Mickey couldn't keep it in any longer. He knew they all despised him, but he couldn't endure their silence any longer; it was killing him.

Larry said, "Don't mind us, Mickey. We're missing Heck, that's all."

"Don't you think I miss him too?" cried Mickey. Afraid he was about to burst into tears, he flung himself from the table and hurried up the stairs to his room. Which used to be Heck's room also.

A short time later there was a knock on the door. It was Larry. "Mind if I come in?"

He sat on the edge of Heck's bed and was silent for a while, his gray head bowed as he studied the knees of his blue jeans. Then he said, "We all liked Heck. Sammy and Jimmy loved him. Candy, too, I think. There was never any real harm in Heck. He didn't always understand everything that was going on around him. But who does? I can't make sense of the world myself. Heck just wanted to please everyone. If he was here right now, I know he wouldn't want you to feel bad about what happened. It wasn't your fault. It was an accident. And Heck was doing what he liked to do best: he was playing a game. It was all a game to Heck. All of it just a big TV show with good guys and bad guys, with Heck one of the good guys. You see?"

"No, I don't see. I'm to blame, Larry. It *was* my fault. I asked him to come. He wouldn't have been there if it wasn't for me. Nothing you can say can change that."

Larry came over and sat beside him. He looped an arm around Mickey's shoulders. "None of us can see the future, Mickey. You had no way of knowing Heck would do what he did. Or that the wood beam would collapse and the wall fall down. He would want you to get on with your life, I know that much."

He stood and moved to the door. He paused. "The other two boys…?"

"Tweed and Bibby."

"How are they doing?"

"They'll be okay. Broken bones, that's all. They were lucky they didn't break their necks."

"You still planning on staying with that Hit Squad of yours?"

Mickey shook his head. "No. The police said it was against the law. And Candy said what we were doing wasn't right. I see that now. The Hit Squad…it was wrong to go after people."

"Candy's got a good head on her shoulders."

"Yeah."

"You want to come down and have your dessert?"

"I can't stand Candy not talking to me."

"She feels bad. You could try talking to her, later maybe, privately."

"What's for dessert?"

Larry frowned. "Some kind of pie Annie made. With ice cream."

Some kind of pie. Anyone would think Larry didn't like Annie's pies, when in fact he couldn't get enough of them. Mickey didn't realize his cheeks were wet until he tried to crack a smile. "I'll be right down."

When he got back to the dining room, Candy had already gone to her room. Sammy and Jimmy were on their second helping of pie. Mickey decided he didn't want dessert after all.

113

He wasn't hungry. He climbed the stairs and knocked on Candy's door. He heard her yell something, so he pushed the door open and stepped inside.

"I said to stay out! I knew it was you."

She was lying on her bed. She had been crying.

"I just want to say that I wish it had been me instead of Heck. Honest, Candy, I mean it."

She sat up, angry, and crying again. "I wish it had been you too! Heck was worth ten of you, Mickey!"

"Yeah. I know." He looked around her room. It wasn't a place he had visited very much. In fact, he couldn't remember the last time he'd been here. Colorful posters on the walls. Her Walkman and a few CDs sat on the top of the dresser. And books. Lots of books.

"So would you mind leaving me alone?"

"I'm sorry, okay?"

She lay down again and closed her eyes.

He left, closing the door behind him.

Chapter Fifteen

The day was wrong for a funeral. Unusually warm, almost like a spring day. A rich smell of grass and newly turned earth. It seemed to Mickey a day for life, not death.

The minister, a tall, lean man in a black robe, spoke about Hector Marmaduke Coggin. Most of what he said was news to Mickey. Heck had lost

his family—parents and two brothers—
in a house fire when he was a small
child. Heck was the only survivor,
rescued by a firefighter. But he suffered
brain damage from the smoke, or from
oxygen deficit.

The minister sprinkled a handful of
dirt onto Heck's coffin. "Ashes to ashes,
dust to dust." His voice carried easily
across the small knot of mourners, the
words dropping and mixing with the air
and the earth and the wreaths of flowers.

Mickey listened to the words and
thought about Heck. Heck didn't even
go to Grandview High, but he had been
the one to die. If Mickey had listened
to Candy, then Heck would still be alive
today. Instead he lay in a box of dark
polished wood, deep in the newly dug
earth. It was hard for Mickey to accept
the idea that while he continued with his
life, poor old Heck would stay here in
the ground, his short life finished.

The minister's words cut into his thoughts.

"...death. To God there are no dead, for in His sight the ones we call dead are still alive. They are still alive and cared for by Him in His kingdom..."

Mickey searched the faces of the other mourners around the graveside. Birgit was beautiful, her blond hair contrasting with her stylish black wool suit. Peter and Whisper were not there. Candy, silent and wet-eyed, in jeans and dark sweater, stood holding a red flower in her hands. The sun behind her glowed off her dark curls to form a halo around her head. The Hobbits, who had been father and mother to Heck, were dry-eyed. But Mickey could see the pain lying deep in their eyes and along the clenched muscles of Larry's jaw.

Why had Peter and Whisper stayed away? Mickey asked himself. He didn't know the answer. Maybe their parents had forbidden them to come. Or maybe they didn't care enough. After all, Heck wasn't their friend.

But Mickey hadn't been much of a friend to Heck either. He had never taken the time to get to know the guy. Had been impatient with him most of the time. He remembered the way Heck was like a puppy, seeking affection.

He looked over at Birgit. Their eyes met. He tried to read them but could see nothing there. To think that just a short time ago those beautiful eyes had bewitched him. Not anymore. Birgit's words—*he's just a big nobody*—still rang in his ears.

Heck's death had changed Mickey, although he didn't fully understand all that was different. He did know that he had been a fool. His need to belong to the Grandview in-group had blinded him. He had never really liked Whisper or Peter. Only Birgit. Or had admired her. Was that the same as liking?

He wasn't sure. But he realized now that Grandview people were no better than anyone else. And that Grandview High was no better than Creekside High.

The minister had stopped speaking. The Hobbits were trickling brown soil through their fingers into the open grave and onto Heck's coffin.

Candy dropped her flower onto the coffin and stood with her head bowed. Then she turned away from the grave-side and headed across the grass toward the cemetery gate.

Mickey turned away from Birgit and hurried after Candy. He fell into step beside her. Her eyes were smudged with tears. "I'm sorry," he said.

"I know you are. But that won't bring Heck back, will it?"

"No."

They walked.

Mickey said, "Are we still friends, Candy?"

"I don't know, Mickey. I don't think I can trust you enough to be a friend. Real friends aren't so stuck on themselves that they always put themselves first. Real friends are thoughtful and kind."

"I could change, Candy. I could change."

Heck's empty chair was filled before the week was out. The Hobbits had a new kid, a fourteen-year-old boy. He had been kicked out of his previous foster home for lighting matches in his room and causing a fire. No one was hurt, but the foster parents said they couldn't take any chances. They had to let him go.

Supper was homemade baked beans and salad. Larry and Annie sat in their usual places at the ends of the table. Mickey sat on one side with the new kid beside him, in Heck's old chair. Candy, Jimmy and Sammy sat opposite.

Jimmy and Sammy couldn't stop staring at the new kid.

It was Candy's turn to say grace. "For what we are about to receive, may the Lord make us thankful."

"Amen," came the response.

"Amen," said Dietrich loudly, several seconds later.

Sammy laughed.

Larry frowned at him.

"Sorry," said Sammy.

Dietrich giggled. "That's all right, Jimmy," he said, smiling at Sammy.

"Sammy," said Sammy. "I'm Sammy." He turned to Jimmy. "This is Jimmy."

The new kid's name was Dietrich Mueller. He was having trouble getting everyone's name straight. He was a student at Grandview. "I seen you at school," Dietrich said to Mickey as he helped himself to the beans. "Beans are good. They make you fart." He giggled loudly.

Mickey looked at the others to see how they were taking this. Jimmy blushed. Sammy laughed and pounded the table with his fist. Candy smiled. Larry frowned at Sammy. Sammy stopped being noisy. Annie had a coughing fit.

When it came to helping himself to the salad, Dietrich dropped the wooden serving fork and spoon. They fell with a clatter onto the table beside Mickey. Dietrich's coordination seemed poor. "Here, let me help," said Mickey, serving him.

"Thanks, Mick," said Dietrich.

"It's Mickey," said Mickey.

"Sorry."

Mickey smiled. "That's okay, Dietrich. You'll soon get used to us."

"At school everyone calls me Deet."

Larry said, "Dietrich is a good name. I hope you won't mind if I call you that, Dietrich?"

"Me too," said Mickey. "I will call you Dietrich."

"We will all call you Dietrich," said Annie.

So that was settled.

Larry said, "We'll need to get you an old bicycle, Dietrich, so you can bike to Grandview with Mickey each day."

Mickey said to Larry and Annie, "I'll be putting in for a transfer back to Creekside." He turned to Dietrich. "You could do the same if you want, Dietrich. We could walk together. It's only a few blocks."

Dietrich looked confused. Then he smiled. "Walk together. I like that."

Mickey looked across at Candy. Her brown eyes were reading his mind again, he could tell. But it was okay; she was smiling her tilted smile back at him.